W9-BTE-122

The Wind in the Willows

KENNETH GRAHAME

Adapted by Bob Blaisdell
Illustrated by Thea Kliros

DOVER PUBLICATIONS, INC.
New York

DOVER CHILDREN'S THRIFT CLASSICS
EDITOR OF THIS VOLUME: CANDACE WARD

Copyright

Copyright © 1995 by Dover Publications, Inc.
All rights reserved under Pan American and International Copyright Conventions.

Published in Canada by General Publishing Company, Ltd., 30 Lesmill Road, Don Mills, Toronto, Ontario.
Published in the United Kingdom by Constable and Company, Ltd., 3 The Lanchesters, 162–164 Fulham Palace Road, London W6 9ER.

Bibliographical Note

This Dover edition, first published in 1995, is a new abridgment, by Bob Blaisdell, of *The Wind in the Willows* (first American publication: Charles Scribner's Sons, New York, 1908). The illustrations and introductory Note have been specially prepared for this edition.

Library of Congress Cataloging-in-Publication Data

Grahame, Kenneth, 1859–1932.
The wind in the willows / Kenneth Grahame ; illustrated by Thea Kliros ; [abridged by Bob Blaisdell].
    p.   cm. — (Dover children's thrift classics)
Summary: The escapades of four animal friends who live along a river in the English countryside—Toad, Mole, Rat, and Badger.
ISBN 0-486-28600-2
[1. Animals—Fiction.] I. Kliros, Thea, ill. II. Blaisdell, Robert. III. Title.
IV. Series.
PZ7.G759Wi   1995
[Fic]—dc20

                               95–6186
                               CIP
                               AC

Manufactured in the United States of America
Dover Publications, Inc., 31 East 2nd Street, Mineola, N.Y. 11501

Note

KENNETH GRAHAME (1859–1932) was born in Edinburgh, Scotland. At the age of four his mother died and, with his three siblings, he moved to a small Berkshire village near the Thames River to live with his grandmother. When he was nine, Grahame was sent to boarding school in Oxford, where he succeeded in academics and athletics. Here, too, Grahame appears to have discovered the River, often exploring the Thames in a canoe. That this love influenced him is clearly seen in *The Wind in the Willows.*

Grahame's most famous work and a classic of children's literature, *The Wind in the Willows* began as a series of bedtime stories created for his son Alastair. The stories began on Alastair's fourth birthday, in 1904, and continued over the next three years.

In 1908 the stories first appeared in book form. They reveal the idyllic country life for which Grahame felt so much nostalgia. With the advent of Toad's motorcar and other inevitable changes, Grahame realized that this life was rapidly disappearing. In the pages of *The Wind in the Willows*, though, Mole, Badger, Water Rat, Toad and all the others live and dream as peacefully as they did when Grahame first introduced them.

Contents

		page
1. The River Bank	....	1
2. The Open Road	....	12
3. The Wild Wood	....	22
4. Mr. Badger	....	32
5. Home, Sweet Home	....	40
6. Mr. Toad	....	46
7. Toad's Adventures	....	55
8. The Further Adventures of Toad	....	67
9. Toad Hall Recaptured	....	77

1

The River Bank

THE MOLE had been working very hard all the morning, spring-cleaning his little home. Spring was moving in the air above and in the earth below and around him, even into his dark and lowly little house.

He suddenly flung down his paint-brush on the floor, said "Bother!" and "O blow!" and also "Hang spring-cleaning!" and bolted out of the house without even waiting to put on his coat. Something up above was calling him, and he made for the steep little tunnel. He scraped and scratched and scrabbled and scrooged, and then he scrooged again and scrabbled and scratched and scraped, working busily with his little paws and muttering to himself, "Up we go! Up we go!" till at last, pop! his snout came out into the sunlight and he found himself rolling in the warm grass of a great meadow.

"This is fine!" he said to himself. The sunshine struck hot on his fur, soft breezes caressed his heated brow, and the songs of happy birds fell on his sensitive hearing. Hither and thither through the meadows he rambled, finding everywhere birds building, flowers budding, leaves thrusting—everything happy and busy. He felt how jolly it was to be the only idle one among all these happy citizens.

He thought his happiness was complete when suddenly he stood by the edge of a full-fed river. Never in his life had he seen a river before. The Mole was bewitched, entranced, fascinated. By the side of the river he trotted, and, when tired at last, he sat on the bank, while the river still chattered on to him.

As he sat on the grass and looked across the river, a dark hole in the bank opposite, just above the water's edge, caught his eye. As he gazed something bright and small seemed to twinkle down in the heart of it, vanished, then twinkled once more like a tiny star. As he looked, it winked at him, and so declared itself to be an eye; and a small face began gradually to grow up round it, like a frame round a picture.

A brown little face, with whiskers.

A round face, with the same twinkle in its eye that had first attracted his notice.

Small neat ears and thick silky hair.

It was the Water Rat!

"Hullo, Mole!" said the Water Rat.

"Hullo, Rat!" said the Mole.

"Would you like to come over?" inquired the Rat. He stooped and unfastened a rope and hauled on it; then he stepped into a little boat. It was painted blue outside and white within, and was just the size for two animals. The Rat paddled across and tied the boat to the bank and invited the Mole aboard.

"This has been a wonderful day!" said the Mole, as the Rat shoved off and took to the oars again. "Do you know I've never been in a boat before in all my life."

"What?" cried the Rat. "Never been in a—you never—what have you been doing, then?"

"Is it so nice as all that?" asked the Mole.

"Nice? It's the *only* thing," said the Water Rat. "Believe me, my young friend, there is *nothing*— absolutely nothing—half so much worth doing as simply going about in boats. Simply going," he said dreamily.

"Look ahead, Rat!" cried the Mole suddenly.

It was too late. The boat struck the bank full tilt. The dreamer lay on his back at the bottom of the boat, his heels in the air. The Rat picked himself up with a pleasant laugh, and said, "Look here! If you've really nothing else on hand this morning, supposing we drop down the river together, and have a long day of it?"

The Mole waggled his toes from sheer happiness. "*What* a day I'm having!" he said. "Let us start at once!"

"Hold hard a minute, then!" said the Rat. He tied the boat to his dock, climbed up into his hole above, and in a few moments reappeared with a fat lunch basket.

"Shove that under your feet," he said to the Mole. He untied the boat and took to his oars again.

"What's inside it?" asked the Mole.

"There's cold chicken inside it," replied the Rat; "coldtonguecoldhamcoldbeefpickledgherkinssaladfrench-rollscresssandwichespottedmeatgingerbeerlemonade-sodawater—"

"O stop, stop," cried the Mole. "This is too much!"

"Do you really think so? It's only what I always take on these little trips."

The Mole, absorbed in the new life he was entering upon, the sparkle, the scents and the sounds and the sunlight, trailed a paw in the water and dreamed long waking dreams.

He asked the Water Rat, "And you really live by the river? What a jolly life!"

"By it and with it and on it and in it," said the Rat. "It's brother and sister to me, and food and drink, and washing. It's my world and I don't want any other. What it hasn't got is not worth having, and what it doesn't know is not worth knowing."

"But isn't it a bit dull at times?" the Mole asked. "Just you and the river, and no one else to pass a word with?"

"No one else to—well, I mustn't be hard on you," said the Rat. "You're new to it, and of course you don't know. The bank is so crowded nowadays that many people are moving away altogether."

"What lies over there?" asked the Mole, waving a paw towards a background of woodland that framed the water-meadows on one side of the river.

"That? O, that's just the Wild Wood," said the Rat. "We don't go there very much, we river-bankers."

"Aren't they—aren't they very *nice* people in there?" said the Mole.

"W-e-ll," said the Rat. "The squirrels are all right. And the rabbits—some of 'em, but rabbits are a mixed lot. And then there's Badger. He lives right in the heart of it; wouldn't live anywhere else. Dear old Badger! Nobody interferes with him. They'd better not."

"Why, who should interfere with him?" asked the Mole.

"Weasels and stoats and foxes and so on. They're all right in a way—but they break out sometimes, and then—well, you can't really trust them, and that's the fact."

"And beyond the Wild Wood?" asked the Mole. "Where it's all blue and dim, and one sees what may be hills and something like the smoke of towns?"

"Beyond the Wild Wood comes the Wide World," said the Rat. "And that's something that doesn't matter, either to you or me. I've never been there, and I'm never going, nor you either, if you've got any sense at all. Don't ever refer to it again, please. Now then! Here's our backwater at last, where we're going to lunch."

Leaving the main stream, they now passed into

what seemed at first sight like a little land-locked lake.

The Rat brought the boat alongside the bank, tied her up, helped the Mole ashore, and swung out the lunch basket. The Mole took out all the mysterious packets one by one from the lunch basket and arranged their contents, gasping, "O my! O my!" at each new item. When all was ready, the Rat said, "Now, pitch in, old fellow!"

After the edge of their hunger was somewhat dulled, the Mole's eyes were able to wander off the tablecloth a little.

A broad glistening muzzle showed itself above the edge of the bank, and the Otter hauled himself out and shook the water from his coat.

"Why didn't you invite me, Ratty?" the Otter asked.

"This was an unplanned party," explained the Rat. "By the way—my friend Mr. Mole."

"Proud, I'm sure," said the Otter, and the two animals were friends ever after. "Such a rumpus everywhere," continued the Otter. "All the world seems out on the river today."

There was a rustle behind them, coming from a hedge, and a stripy head, with high shoulders behind it, peered forth on them.

"Come on, old Badger!" shouted the Rat.

The Badger trotted forward a pace or two; then grunted, "H'm! Company," and turned his back and disappeared from view.

"That's just the sort of fellow he is!" observed the

Rat. "Simply hates society! Now we shan't see any more of him today. Well, tell us, Otter, who's out on the river?"

"Toad's out, for one," replied the Otter. "In his brand-new boat."

From where they sat they could get a glimpse of the main stream across the island. And just then the new boat flashed into view—the rower splashing badly and rolling a good deal, but working his hardest. The Rat stood up and hailed him, but Toad shook his head and continued to row.

Shortly after, the Otter spotted a May-fly and swooped into the water after it.

"Well, well," said the Rat, "I suppose we ought to be moving."

The Mole packed up the lunch basket and they got back in the Rat's little boat.

The afternoon sun was getting low as the Rat rowed gently homewards. The Mole was very full of lunch, and already quite at home in a boat (so he thought) and was getting a bit restless besides. He said, "Ratty! Please, *I* want to row now!"

The Rat shook his head with a smile. "Not yet, my young friend," he said. "Wait till you've had a few lessons. It's not so easy as it looks."

The Mole was quiet for a minute or two. But he began to feel more and more jealous of Rat, rowing so strongly and easily along, and he imagined that he could do it every bit as well. He jumped up and seized the oars, so suddenly that the Rat, who was gazing out over the water and saying poetry-things to himself, was taken by surprise and fell backwards off his seat with his legs in the air for the second time, while the triumphant Mole took his place and grabbed the oars with entire confidence.

"Stop it, you silly fool!" cried the Rat, from the bottom of the boat. "You can't do it! You'll have us over!"

The Mole flung his oars back, and made a great dig at the water. He missed the surface altogether, his legs flew up above his head, and he found himself lying on the top of the tumbled Rat. He made a grab at the side of the boat, and the next moment— Sploosh!

Over went the boat, and he found himself struggling in the river.

The Rat hauled the Mole out of the water, and set him down on the bank, a squashy lump of misery.

When all was ready for a start once more, the Mole, limp and dejected, took his seat in the stern of the boat; and as they set off, he said, "Ratty, my generous friend! I am very sorry indeed for my foolish and ungrateful conduct."

"That's all right," responded the Rat cheerily. "What's a little wet to a Water Rat? I'm more in the water than out of it most days. Look here, I really think you had better come and stay with me for a little time. I'll teach you to row, and to swim."

The Mole was so touched by his kind manner of speaking that he could find no voice to answer him; and he had to brush away a tear or two with the back of his paw.

When they got home, the Rat made a bright fire in the parlor, and planted the Mole in an armchair in front of it, and told him river stories till suppertime. Supper was a most cheerful meal; but very shortly afterwards a terribly sleepy Mole had to be escorted upstairs by his considerate host, to the best bedroom, where he soon laid his head on his pillow in great peace and contentment, knowing that his new-found friend the River was lapping the sill of his window.

This day was only the first of many similar ones for the Mole, each of them longer and full of interest as the spring became summer. He learnt to swim and to row, and entered into the joy of the River; and listening to the reeds by the riverside, he caught, sometimes, something of what the wind went whispering so constantly among them.

2

The Open Road

"RATTY," SAID the Mole one bright summer morning, "if you please, I want to ask you a favor. Won't you take me to call on Mr. Toad? I've heard so much about him, and I do so want to meet him."

"Why, certainly," said the Rat. "Get the boat out and we'll paddle up there. It's never the wrong time to call on Toad. Early or late, he's always the same fellow. Always glad to see you, always sorry when you go! . . . It may be that he is both boastful and conceited. But he has got some great qualities, has Toady."

Rounding a bend in the river, they came in sight of a handsome, old house of red brick and lawns reaching down to the water's edge.

"There's Toad Hall," said the Rat. "Toad is rather rich, you know, and this is really one of the nicest houses in these parts."

They got out of Rat's boat and strolled across the pretty flower-decked lawns in search of Toad, whom they soon found resting in a garden chair, with a far-off look in his eyes, and a large map spread out on his knees.

"Hooray!" he cried, jumping up on seeing them, "this is splendid!" He shook the paws of both of them. "How *kind* of you!" he went on dancing round them. "I was just going to send a boat down the river for you, Ratty. I want you badly—both of you. Come inside and have something!"

"Let's sit quiet a bit, Toady!" said the Rat.

"You are the very animals I wanted. You've got to help me. It's most important," said Toad.

"It's about your rowing, I suppose," said the Rat. "You're getting on fairly well, though you splash a good bit still."

"O, pooh! boating!" said the Toad. "Silly boyish amusement. No, I've discovered the real thing. I propose to devote the remainder of my lifetime to it. Come with me, dear Ratty, and your nice friend also, just as far as the stableyard, and you shall see what you shall see!"

Toad led the way, and there, outside the coach house in the open, they saw a horse-drawn caravan, shining with newness, painted yellow with green and red wheels.

"There you are!" cried the Toad. "There's real life for you. The open road, the dusty highway, the countryside! Camps, villages, towns, cities! Here today, up and off to somewhere else tomorrow. Travel, change, interest, excitement! The whole world before you, and a horizon that's always changing!"

The van was indeed very compact and comfortable. Little sleeping bunks, a little table, a cooking-stove, lockers, bookshelves, a birdcage with a bird in it; and pots, pans, jugs and kettles of every size.

"All complete!" said the Toad. "You see—biscuits, canned lobster and sardines—everything you could possibly want. You'll find that nothing whatever has been forgotten, when we make our start this afternoon."

"I beg your pardon," said the Rat. "But did I overhear you say something about *'we,'* and *'start,'* and *'this afternoon'*?"

"Now, you dear good old Ratty," said Toad, "you know you've got to come. I can't possibly manage without you. You surely don't mean to stick to your dull old river all your life, and just live in a hole in a bank, and boat? I want to show you the world!"

"I don't care," said the Rat. "I'm not coming. And I *am* going to stick to my old river, *and* live in a hole, *and* boat, as I've always done. And what's more,

Mole's going to stick to me and do as I do, aren't you, Mole?"

"Of course I am," said the Mole. "I'll always stick to you, Rat, and what you say is to be—has got to be. All the same, it sounds as if it might have been—well, rather fun, you know!"

"Come along in, and have some lunch," said Toad, "and we'll talk it over. Of course, I don't really care. I only want to give pleasure to you fellows. 'Live for others!' That's my motto in life."

During lunch, which was excellent, of course, it soon seemed taken for granted by all three of them that the trip was a settled thing; the Rat could not bear to disappoint his two friends, who were already deep in plans for each day's activities of several weeks ahead.

When they were quite ready that afternoon, the Toad led his companions to the paddock and set them to capture the old gray horse. In the meantime, Toad packed the caravan lockers still tighter with necessities. At last the horse was caught, and they set off, all talking at once, each animal either trudging by the side of the cart or sitting on the shaft. It was a golden afternoon. On either side of the road, birds called and whistled to them; pleasant wayfarers gave them "Good day," or stopped to say nice things about their beautiful cart; and rabbits, sitting at their front doors in the hedgerows, held up their forepaws and said, "O my! O my! O my!"

Late in the evening, miles from home, they drew up

on a remote meadow, turned the horse loose to graze, and ate their simple supper sitting on the grass by the side of the cart. Toad talked big about all he was going to do in the days to come, while stars grew fuller and larger all around them, and a yellow moon came to keep them company and listen to their talk. At last they turned in to their little bunks in the caravan; and Toad said, "Well, good night, you fellows! This is the real life for a gentleman! Talk about your old river!"

"I *don't* talk about my river," replied the Rat. "You *know* I don't, Toad. But I *think* about it. I think about it—all the time!"

The Mole reached out from under his blanket, felt for the Rat's paw in the darkness, and gave it a squeeze. "I'll do whatever you like, Ratty," he whispered. "Shall we run away tomorrow morning, quite early, and go back to our dear old hole on the river?"

"No, no, we'll see it out," whispered back the Rat. "Thanks awfully, but I ought to stick by Toad till this trip is ended. It wouldn't be safe for him to be left to himself. It won't take very long. His fads never do. Good night!"

The end was indeed nearer than even the Rat suspected.

They had a pleasant ramble that next day over grassy hills, and along narrow side roads, and camped as before.

The following afternoon was when they came out on the main road, their first main road; and their disaster, fleet and unforeseen, sprang out on them.

They were driving along easily, the Mole by the horse's head, talking to him, since the horse had complained that he was being left out of it, and nobody considered him in the least; the Toad and the Water Rat walking behind the cart talking together. Far behind them they heard a faint warning hum, like the drone of a distant bee. Glancing back, they saw a small cloud of dust advancing on them at incredible speed, while from out of the dust a faint "Poop-poop!" wailed. In an instant the peaceful scene was changed, and with a blast of wind and a whirl of sound that made them jump for the nearest ditch, it was on them! The "Poop-poop" rang with a shout in their ears, and the magnificent motorcar, with its driver tense and hugging his wheel, possessed all the earth and air for a fraction of a second, flung a cloud of dust that blinded and enwrapped them utterly, and then dwindled to a speck in the far distance, changing back into a droning bee once more.

The old gray horse reared and plunged, in spite of all the Mole's efforts at his head, and drove the cart backward towards the deep ditch at the side of the road. A moment later, the yellow cart, their pride and joy, lay on its side in the ditch, a wreck.

The Rat danced up and down in the road. "You villains!" he shouted, shaking both fists. "You scoundrels, you highwaymen, you—you—roadhogs!—I'll have the law on you! I'll report you! I'll take you through all the courts!"

Toad sat straight down in the middle of the dusty

road, his legs stretched out before him, and stared in the direction of the disappearing motorcar. Every so often he faintly murmured, "Poop-poop!" Rat and Mole found him in a sort of trance, a happy smile on his face. He was still faintly murmuring, "Poop-poop!"

The Rat shook him by the shoulder. "Are you coming to help us, Toad?"

"Glorious, stirring sight!" murmured Toad, not moving. "The poetry of motion! The *real* way to travel. The *only* way to travel! O bliss! O poop-poop! O my! O my!"

"O stop being a fool, Toad!" cried the Mole.

"And to think I never knew!" went on the Toad. "All those wasted years. I never knew, I never even dreamt! O what a flowery track lies spread before me now!

What dust clouds shall spring up behind me as I
speed on my reckless way!"

"What are we to do with him?" asked the Mole of
the Water Rat.

"Nothing at all," replied the Rat. "He is now possessed. He has got a new craze, and it always takes
him that way, in its first stage. Now, look here, Toad!"
said the Rat sharply. "As soon as we get to the town,
you'll have to go straight to the police station, and
see if they know anything about the motorcar and
who it belongs to, and lodge a complaint against it."

"Police station! Complaint!" said Toad. "Me com-
plain of that beautiful, that heavenly vision! I've done
with carts forever. I never want to see the caravan, or
to hear of it again. O Ratty! You can't think how
obliged I am to you for consenting to come on this
trip! I wouldn't have gone without you. I might never
have heard that entrancing sound, or smelt that be-
witching smell!"

Rat turned to the Mole and said, "He's quite hope-
less. I give it up—when we get to the town we'll go to
the railway station."

Eventually, a slow train having landed them all at a
station not very far from Toad Hall, they escorted
Toad to his door, put him inside it, and instructed his
housekeeper to feed him, undress him, and put him
to bed. Then they got out their boat and rowed down
the river home, and at a very late hour sat down to
supper in their own cozy riverside parlor, to the Rat's
great joy and contentment.

The following evening the Mole was sitting on the bank fishing, when the Rat came strolling along to find him. "Heard the news?" he said. "Toad went up to town by an early train this morning. And he has ordered a large and very expensive motorcar."

3
The Wild Wood

WHENEVER THE Mole mentioned his wish to meet the Badger to the Water Rat he always found himself put off. "It's all right," the Rat would say. "Badger'll turn up some day or other—he's always turning up—and then I'll introduce you."

"Couldn't you ask him here—dinner or something?" said the Mole.

"He wouldn't come," replied the Rat. "Badger hates society, and invitations, and dinner, and all that sort of thing."

"Well, then, supposing we go and call on *him?*" suggested the Mole.

"O, I'm sure he wouldn't like that at *all,*" said the Rat. "He's so very shy, he'd be sure to be offended. Besides, we can't. It's quite out of the question, because he lives in the very middle of the Wild Wood. He'll be coming along some day, if you'll wait quietly."

But the Badger never came along, and every day brought its amusements, and it was not till summer was long over, and cold and frost and muddy ways kept them much indoors, and the swollen river raced past outside their windows with a speed that made boating impossible, that the Mole found himself thinking again about the shy Badger, who lived his own life by himself, in his hole in the middle of the Wild Wood.

There was plenty to talk about on those short winter days when the animals found themselves round the fire; still, the Mole had a good deal of spare time on his hands, and so one afternoon, when the Rat was dozing in his armchair before the fire, he decided to go out by himself and explore the Wild Wood, and perhaps meet Mr. Badger.

It was a cold afternoon when he slipped out of the warm parlor into the open air. The country lay bare and leafless around him, but with great cheerfulness he pushed on towards the Wild Wood.

There was nothing to alarm him at first entry, but he went further to where the light was less, and trees crouched nearer and nearer. The dusk came on rapidly, and the light seemed to be draining away like flood water.

Then the faces began.

It was over his shoulder that he first thought he saw a face; a little wedge-shaped face, looking out at him from a hole. When he turned and confronted it, the thing had vanished.

He quickened his pace, telling himself not to begin imagining things. He passed another hole, and another, and another; and then—yes!—no!—yes! certainly a little narrow face, with hard eyes, had flashed up for an instant from a hole, and was gone.

If he could only get away from the holes in the banks, he thought, there would be no more faces. He swung off the path and plunged into the wood.

Then the whistling began.

Very faint and shrill it was; and far behind him, when he first heard it; but somehow it made him hurry forward. Then, it sounded far ahead of him, and made him hesitate and want to go back. As he halted, it broke out on either side, and seemed to be caught up and passed on throughout the whole length of the wood to its farthest limit.

He was alone and far from any help; and the night was closing in.

Then the pattering began.

It increased until it sounded like sudden hail on the dry leaf-carpet spread around him. The whole wood seemed running now, running hard, hunting,

chasing, closing in round something or—somebody? In panic, he began to run too, aimlessly, he did not know where. He ran up against things and dodged round things and into things; he darted under things. At last he took refuge in a deep dark hollow of an old beech tree. As he lay there panting and trembling, and listened to the whistlings and the patterings outside, he knew it at last, in all its fullness—the Terror of the Wild Wood!

Meantime the Rat, warm and comfortable, dozed by his fireside. When he woke up and then looked round for the Mole, he was not there.

He listened for a time. The house seemed very quiet.

Then he called, "Moly!" several times, and receiving no answer, got up and went out into the hall.

The Mole's cap was missing from its peg. His

galoshes, which always lay by the umbrella stand, were also gone.

The Rat left the house, and carefully examined the muddy surface of the ground outside, hoping to find the Mole's tracks. There they were, sure enough. He could see the imprints of the galoshes in the mud, running along straight and purposeful, leading direct to the Wild Wood.

The Rat looked very grave, and stood in deep thought for a minute or two. Then he reentered the house, strapped a belt round his waist, shoved a pair of pistols into it, took up a thick stick that stood in the corner of the hall, and set off for the Wild Wood.

He made his way bravely through the length of the wood, to its furthest edge; then, leaving behind all paths, he set himself to cross it, all the time calling out, "Moly, Moly, Moly! Where are you? It's me—it's old Rat!"

He had hunted through the wood for an hour when at last to his joy he heard a little answering cry. Guiding himself by the sound, he made his way through the gathering darkness to the foot of an old beech tree, with a hole in it, and from out of the hole came a feeble voice, saying "Ratty! Is that really you?"

The Rat crept into the hollow, and there he found the Mole, exhausted and still trembling. "O Rat!" the Mole cried, "I've been so frightened!"

"O, I quite understand," said the Rat soothingly. "You really shouldn't have gone and done it, Mole. I did my best to keep you from it. We river-bankers, we hardly ever come here by ourselves."

"Surely the brave Mr. Toad wouldn't mind coming here by himself, would he?" asked the Mole.

"Old Toad?" said the Rat, laughing. "He wouldn't show his face here alone, not for a whole hatful of gold. Now then, we really must make a start for home."

"Dear Ratty," said the Mole, "you must let me rest here a while longer, and get my strength back, if I'm to get home at all."

"O, all right," said the Rat, "rest away."

So the Mole got well into the dry leaves within the hole in the beech and dropped off to sleep, while the Rat covered himself up, too, for warmth, and lay waiting, with a pistol in his paw.

When at last the Mole woke up, the Rat said, "I'll just take a look outside and see if everything's quiet, and then we really must be off."

He went to the entrance of their retreat and put his head out. "It's snowing hard," he announced.

The Mole came and crouched beside him, and, looking out, saw the wood that had been so dreadful to him. A gleaming carpet of snow was springing up everywhere. A fine powder filled the air and caressed the cheek with a tingle in its touch.

"Well, well, it can't be helped," said the Rat. "We must make a start, and take our chances, I suppose. The worst of it is, I don't exactly know where we are.

And now this snow makes everything look so very different."

An hour or two later—they had lost all count of time—they pulled up, weary, and hopelessly at sea, and sat down on a fallen tree trunk to recover their breath and consider what was to be done. The snow was getting so deep that they could hardly drag their little legs through it, and the trees were thicker and more like each other than ever.

"We can't sit here very long," said the Rat. "There's a sort of dell down here in front of us, where the ground seems all hilly and humpy. We'll make our way down into that, and try and find some sort of shelter, a cave or hole with a dry floor to it."

So once more they got on their feet, and struggled down into the dell. Suddenly, the Mole tripped and fell forward on his face with a squeal.

"O my leg!" he cried. "O my poor shin!" and he sat up on the snow and nursed his leg in both his front paws.

"It's a very clean cut," said the Rat, examining it. "That was never done by a branch or a stump. It looks as if it was made by a sharp edge of something in metal."

"Well, never mind what done it," said the Mole, forgetting his grammar. "It hurts just the same, whatever done it."

But the Rat, after carefully tying up the leg with his handkerchief, had left Mole and was busy scraping in the snow.

Suddenly the Rat cried "Hooray!" and then "Hooray-oo-ray-oo-ray-oo-ray!" and did a little dance. "Come and see!" said the delighted Rat.

The Mole hobbled up to the spot and had a good look. "A door-scraper! Well, what of it? Why dance jigs around a door-scraper?"

"But don't you see what it *means*, you—you dull-witted animal?" cried the Rat.

"It simply means that some *very* careless and forgetful person has left his door-scraper lying about in the middle of the Wild Wood, *just* where it's *sure* to trip *everybody* up."

"O, dear! O, dear!" cried the Rat. "Stop arguing and come and scrape!" He set to work again and made the snow fly in all directions.

After some further toil, a very shabby doormat lay exposed to view.

"There, what did I tell you?" exclaimed the Rat.

"Well now," said the Mole, "you seem to have found another piece of litter, done for and thrown away, and I suppose you're perfectly happy. Go ahead and dance your jig round that, and then perhaps we can go on and not waste any more time over rubbish heaps. Can we eat a doormat? Or sleep under a doormat? Or sit on a doormat and sledge home over the snow on it, you exasperating rodent?"

"Do—you—mean—to—say," cried the Rat, "that this doormat doesn't *tell* you anything?"

"Really, Rat," said the Mole, "I think we've had enough of this silliness. Who ever heard of a doormat *telling* anyone anything?"

"Now look here, you—you thick-headed beast," replied the Rat, "this must stop. Not another word from you, but scrape—scrape and scratch and dig and hunt round, if you want to sleep dry and warm tonight, for it's our last chance!"

The Rat attacked a snowbank with his big stick and then dug with fury; and the Mole scraped busily too, more to oblige the Rat than for any other reason.

After ten minutes' hard work, the point of the Rat's stick struck something that sounded hollow. He called the Mole to come help him.

In the side of what seemed to be a snowbank stood a solid-looking little door, painted a dark green. An iron bellpull hung by the side, and below it, on a small brass plate, they could read by the aid of moonlight: "MR. BADGER."

The Mole fell backwards on the snow from sheer surprise and delight. "Rat!" he cried in apology, "you're a wonder! I see it all now! You're so clever, I believe you could find anything you liked."

While the Rat attacked the door now with his stick, the Mole sprang up at the bellpull, clutched it and swung there, both feet well off the ground, and from quite a long way off they could faintly hear a bell respond.

4

Mr. Badger

THEY WAITED for what seemed a very long time, stamping in the snow to keep their feet warm. At last there was the noise of a bolt shot back, and the door opened a few inches, enough to show a long snout and a pair of sleepy blinking eyes.

"Who is it, disturbing people on such a night? Speak up!" said a gruff voice.

"O, Badger," cried the Rat, "let us in, please. It's me, Rat, and my friend Mole, and we've lost our way in the snow."

"What, Ratty, my dear little man!" exclaimed the Badger. "Come along in, both of you, at once. Lost in the snow! And in the Wild Wood, too, and at this time of night! But come in with you."

The Badger, who wore a long dressing gown, carried a candlestick in his paw and had probably been on his way to bed. He patted both their heads. "This is not the sort of night for small animals to be out," he said. "But come along; come into the kitchen. There's a first-rate fire there, and supper."

He shuffled in front of them, carrying the light, and they followed him, nudging each other, down a long, gloomy passage, into a central hall, out of which they could dimly see other long tunnel-like passages branching, passages mysterious and without apparent end. But there were doors in the hall as well—sturdy oaken doors. One of these the Badger flung open, and at once they found themselves in all the glow and warmth of a large firelit kitchen.

The kindly Badger thrust them down on a bench by the fire, and asked them to remove their wet coats and boots. Then he fetched them dressing gowns and slippers, and himself bathed the Mole's shin with warm water and mended the cut with plaster till the whole thing was as good as new, if not better.

It seemed to the Rat and the Mole, now in this safe place, that the cold and trackless Wild Wood they had just left outside was miles and miles away, and that they had suffered in it a half-forgotten dream.

When at last they were thoroughly toasted, the Badger summoned them to the table, where he had been busy laying out a meal.

The Badger sat in his armchair at the head of the table, and nodded as the animals ate and told their story; and he did not seem surprised or shocked at anything, and he never said, "I told you so," or, "Just what I always said," or remarked that they ought to have done so-and-so, or ought not to have done something else. The Mole began to feel very friendly towards him.

When supper was finished, they gathered round the glowing embers of the great wood fire, and thought how jolly it was to be sitting up so late, and so full, and after they chatted for a time about things in general, the Badger asked, "How's old Toad going on?"

"O, from bad to worse," said the Rat. "Another smash-up only last week, and a bad one. You see, he insists on driving himself, and he's hopelessly incapable. He's convinced he's a heaven-born driver, and nobody can teach him anything."

"How many has he had?" asked the Badger.

"Smashes, or motorcars?" replied the Rat. "O, well, after all, it's the same thing—with Toad. This is the seventh."

"He's been in the hospital three times," added the Mole.

"He's a hopelessly bad driver," went on the Rat,

"and quite regardless of law and order. Killed or ruined—it's got to be one of the two things, sooner or later. Badger, we're his friends—oughtn't we to do something?"

"Of course you know I can't do anything *now*," said the Badger. No animal, according to the rules of the animal world, is ever expected to do anything difficult, or heroic, or even very active during the off-season of winter. All are sleepy—some actually asleep. All are weatherbound, more or less. "But, when once the year has really turned and the nights are shorter, we'll take Toad seriously in hand. We'll make him be a sensible Toad. We'll—you're asleep, Rat!"

"Not me!" said the Rat, waking up.

"He's been asleep two or three times since supper," said the Mole, laughing. He himself was feeling quite wakeful and even lively. The reason was that he being naturally an underground animal by birth and breeding, the situation of Badger's house exactly suited him and made him feel at home; while the Rat, who slept every night in a bedroom the windows of which opened on a breezy river, naturally felt the atmosphere still and oppressive.

"Well, it's time we were all in bed," said the Badger. "Come along, you two, and I'll show you your quarters."

The two tired little animals came down to breakfast very late next morning, and found a bright fire burning

in the kitchen, and two young hedgehogs sitting on a bench at the table, eating oatmeal out of wooden bowls.

The Rat greeted the young school-age hedgehogs and then asked, "What's the weather like outside?"

"O, terrible bad, sir, terrible deep the snow is," said the elder of the two hedgehogs. "No getting out for the likes of you gentlemen today."

"Where's Mr. Badger?" asked the Mole.

"The master's gone into his study, sir," replied the hedgehog, "and he said he was going to be particularly busy this morning, and on no account was he to be disturbed."

The animals well knew that Badger, having eaten a hearty breakfast, had gone to his study and settled himself in an armchair with his legs up on another and a red cotton handkerchief over his face, and was being "busy" in the usual way at this time of the year.

The front-door bell clanged loudly, and the Rat, who was very greasy with buttered toast, sent Billy, the smaller hedgehog, to see who it might be. In a few moments Billy returned in front of the Otter, who threw himself on the Rat in a friendly greeting.

"Get off!" spluttered the Rat.

"I thought I should find you here all right," said the Otter. "They were all in a great alarm along the River Bank when I arrived this morning. Rat never been home all night—nor Mole either—something dreadful must have happened, they said; and the snow had covered up all your tracks, of course. But I knew that when people were in any fix they mostly went to Badger, or else Badger got to know of it somehow, so I came off straight here, through the Wild Wood and the snow! My, it was fine, coming through the snow as the red sun was rising and showing against the black tree trunks!"

"Weren't you nervous?" asked the Mole.

"Nervous?" The Otter showed a gleaming set of strong white teeth as he laughed.

During lunch, while the Rat and the Otter talked together, Mole found himself placed next to Mr. Badger. He told Badger how comfortable and home-like it all felt to him. "Once well underground," he said, "you know exactly where you are. Nothing can happen to you, and nothing can get at you. You're entirely your own master, and you don't have to consult anybody or mind what they say. Things go on all the same overhead, and you let 'em, and don't bother about 'em. When you want to, up you go, and there the things are, waiting for you."

The Badger simply beamed on him. "That's exactly what I say," he replied. "There's no security, or peace and tranquility, except underground. And then, if your ideas get larger and you want to expand—why, a dig and a scrape, and there you are! If you feel your house is a bit too big, you stop up a hole or two, and there you are again. And, above all, no *weather*. No, up and out of doors is good enough to roam about in; but underground to come back to at last—that's my idea of *home!*" The Badger was pleased with the Mole, who agreed with him. "When lunch is over," he said, "I'll take you all round this little place of mine. I can see you'll appreciate it."

When they got back from their tour, they found the Rat walking up and down, very restless. The underground atmosphere was getting on his nerves, and he seemed really to be afraid that the river would run away if he wasn't there to look after it.

"Come along, Mole," he said, as soon as he caught sight of him. "We must get off while it's daylight."

"It'll be all right, my fine fellow," said the Otter. "I'm coming along with you, and I know every path blindfolded."

"You really needn't fret, Ratty," added the Badger. "My passages run further than you think, and I've holes to the edge of the wood in several directions. You shall leave by one of my shortcuts."

The Badger led the way along a damp and airless tunnel that wound and dipped for a long distance. At last, daylight began to show itself through the growth overhanging the mouth of the passage; and the Badger, bidding them goodbye, pushed them through the opening, made everything look as natural as possible again, and retreated.

They found themselves standing on the very edge of the Wild Wood. They made swiftly for home, for firelight and the familiar things it played on, for the voice of the river that they knew and trusted, that never made them afraid.

5

Home, Sweet Home

ONE DAY that winter the Mole and the Water Rat were returning across country after a long day's outing with Otter, hunting and exploring the lands surrounding the streams that fed into their own river. On either side of the road past the village they could smell through the darkness the friendly fields again. They plodded along silently, each of them thinking his own thoughts. Suddenly a feeling went through the Mole. He stopped in his tracks, his nose searching here and there to catch the current of Home that called him, those invisible little hands pulling and tugging, all one way. Why, it must be quite close by him at that moment, his old home that he had forsaken and never looked for again, since that day when he first found the river!

Shabby indeed, and small and poorly furnished, and yet his, the home he had made for himself, the home he had been so happy to get back to after his day's work. And the home had been happy with him, too, evidently, and was missing him, and wanted him back, and was telling him so, through his nose.

The call was clear. He must obey it instantly, and go. "Ratty!" he called, "hold on! Come back! I want you, quick!"

"Oh, *come* along, Mole, do!" replied the Rat, still plodding along.

"*Please* stop, Ratty!" pleaded the poor Mole. "You don't understand! It's my home, my old home! I've just come across the smell of it. And I *must* go to it, I must."

"Mole, we mustn't stop now, really!" said the Rat. "We'll come for it tomorrow, whatever it is you've found. The snow's coming on again." The Rat pressed forward without waiting for an answer.

Poor Mole stood alone in the road, his heart torn in two. But even under such a test as this his loyalty to his friend stood firm. He followed obediently in the track of the Rat.

But finally, after Mole caught up to Rat, a sob forced its way through Mole, and he cried helplessly.

The Rat, astonished and dismayed, said very quietly and nicely, "What is it, old fellow? Whatever can be the matter? Tell us your trouble, and let me see what I can do."

"I know it's a—shabby, dark little place," he

sobbed, "not like—your cozy quarters—or Toad's beautiful hall—or Badger's great house—but it was my own little home—and I was fond of it—and I went away and forgot all about it—and then I smelt it suddenly—on the road, when I called and you wouldn't listen, Rat—and everything came back to me with a rush—and I wanted it!—O dear, O dear!— and when you wouldn't turn back, Ratty—and I had to leave it, though I was smelling it all the time—I thought my heart would break.—We might have gone and had one look at it, Ratty—only one look—it was close by—but you wouldn't turn back, Ratty, you wouldn't turn back! O dear, O dear!"

The Rat patted Mole gently on the shoulder. After a time Rat muttered, "I see it all now! What a *pig* I have been! A pig—that's me! Just a pig—a plain pig!" Then he rose from his seat and remarking, "Well, now we'd really better be getting on, old chap!" set off up the road the way they had come.

"Wherever are you going to, Ratty?" said the tearful Mole.

"We're going to find that home of yours, old fellow," replied the Rat. "So you had better come along, for we shall want your nose."

When at last it seemed to the Rat that they must be nearing that part of the road where the Mole had been held up, he said, "Now, use your nose, and give your mind to it."

Mole stood a moment rigid, while his uplifted nose, quivering slightly, felt the air.

The Rat, much excited, kept close to his heels as the Mole, with something of the air of a sleepwalker, crossed a dry ditch, scrambled through a hedge, and nosed his way over a field open and trackless and bare in the faint starlight.

Suddenly, without warning, he dived; but the Rat was on the alert, and promptly followed him down the tunnel to which his nose had led him.

It was close and airless within, and the earthy smell was strong, and it seemed a long time to Rat before the passage ended and he could stand up and stretch and shake himself. The Mole struck a match, and by its light the Rat saw that directly facing them was Mole's little front door, with "Mole End" painted over the bellpull at the side.

Mole hurried Rat through the door, lit a lamp in the hall, and took one glance round his old home. He

saw the dust lying thick on everything, saw the deserted look of the long-neglected house, and its narrowness, its worn and shabby contents—and collapsed on a hall chair, his nose to his paws. "O Ratty!" he cried. "Why did I ever bring you to this poor, cold little place, on a night like this, when you might have been at River Bank by this time, toasting your toes before a blazing fire, with all your own nice things about you!"

The Rat paid no attention to the Mole's words. He was running here and there, opening doors, inspecting rooms and cupboards, and lighting lamps and candles. "What a capital little house this is!" he called out. "So compact! So well planned! Everything here and everything in its place! We'll make a jolly night of it."

The Mole roused himself but soon had another fit of the blues. "Rat," he moaned, "how about your supper, you poor, cold, hungry, weary animal. I've nothing to give you—nothing—not a crumb!"

"Pull yourself together, Mole, and come with me and forage."

They went and foraged, hunting through every cupboard and turning out every drawer. The result was not so depressing after all: a tin of sardines, a box of biscuits and a German sausage encased in silver paper.

"There's a banquet for you!" said the Rat, as he arranged the table. "I know some animals who would give their ears to be sitting down to supper with us tonight!"

"No bread!" groaned the Mole, "no butter, no—"

"No caviar, no champagne!" continued the Rat, teasing Mole.

After they ate, Mole and Rat kicked the fire up, drew their chairs in, brewed themselves a last drink of hot cider, and discussed the events of the long day. At last the Rat, with a tremendous yawn, said, "Mole, old chap, I'm ready to drop. Sleepy is simply not the word. Is that your own bank over on that side? Very well, then, I'll take this. What a fine little house this is! Everything so handy!"

The weary Mole also was glad to turn in without delay, and soon had his head on his pillow, in great joy and contentment. He saw how plain and simple his home all was; but clearly, too, how much it all meant to him. He did not at all want to abandon the new life and its splendid spaces, to turn his back on sun and air and all they offered him and creep home and stay there; the upper world was all too strong, it called to him still, even down there, and he knew he must return to the larger stage. But it was good to think he had this to come back to, this place which was all his own, these things which were so glad to see him again and could always be counted upon for the same simple welcome.

6

Mr. Toad

IT WAS a bright morning in the early part of summer; a hot sun seemed to be pulling everything green and bushy and spiky up out of the earth towards him. The Mole and the Water Rat had been up since dawn, very busy on matters connected with boats and the opening of the boating season. They were finishing breakfast in their little parlor when a heavy knock sounded at the door.

The Mole opened the door. "Mr. Badger!"

The Badger walked into the room and stood looking at the two animals with a serious expression.

"The hour has come!" said the Badger.

"What hour?" asked the Rat.

"Whose hour, you should say," replied the Badger. "Why, Toad's hour! I said I would take him in hand as soon as the winter was well over, and I'm going to give him his lesson today!"

"Hooray," cried the Mole. "I remember now! *We'll* teach him to be a sensible Toad!"

They reached the driveway of Toad Hall to find, as the Badger had guessed, a shiny new motorcar, of great size, painted a bright red (Toad's favorite color), standing in front of the house. As they neared the door it was flung open, and Mr. Toad, arrayed in goggles, cap and enormous overcoat, came swaggering down the steps, drawing on his gloves.

"Hullo! come on, you fellows!" he cried. "You're just in time to come with me for a jolly—" He had noticed the stern look on the faces of his friends, and his invitation remained unfinished.

The Badger walked up the steps. "Take him inside," he said to his companions. Toad was hustled through the door, struggling and protesting. Badger followed and shut the door.

"Now then," Badger said, "first of all, take those ridiculous things off!"

"I shan't!" replied Toad. "What is the meaning of this?"

"Take them off him, then, you two," ordered the Badger.

The Rat sat on Toad, and the Mole got his motorcar clothes off him bit by bit, and they stood him up on his legs again. Now that he was merely Toad, and no longer the Terror of the Highway, he giggled and looked from one to the other.

"You knew it must come to this, sooner or later, Toad," the Badger explained. "You've disregarded all the warnings we've given you, you've gone on squandering the money your father left you, and you're getting us animals a bad name by your furious driving and your smashes and your fights with the police. We animals never allow our friends to make fools of themselves beyond a certain limit; and that limit you've reached. You will come with me into the next room, and there you will hear some facts about yourself; and we'll see whether you come out of that room the same Toad that you went in."

He took Toad by the arm, led him into the next room, and closed the door behind them.

"That's no good!" said the Rat. "*Talking* to Toad'll never cure him."

After almost an hour, the door opened and the Badger reappeared, leading by the paw a very limp and dejected Toad.

"Sit down there, Toad," said the Badger, pointing to a chair. "My friends," he went on, "I am pleased to inform you that Toad has at last seen the error of his ways. He is truly sorry for his misguided conduct in the past, and he has undertaken to give up motorcars entirely and forever. I have his promise."

"That is very good news," said the Mole.

"Very good news indeed," said the Rat, "if only—if only—"

"There's only one thing more to be done," said the Badger. "Toad, I want you to repeat, before your friends here, what you admitted to me in the other room just now. First, you are sorry for what you've done, and you see the folly of it all?"

There was a long, long pause. Toad looked this way and that, and at last he spoke. "No!" he said. "I'm *not* sorry. And it wasn't folly at all! It was simply glorious!"

"What?" cried the Badger. "You backsliding animal, didn't you tell me just now, in there—"

"Oh, yes, yes, in *there,*" said Toad. "But I've been searching my mind since, and I find that I'm not a bit sorry really, so it's no good saying I am; now, is it?"

"Then you don't promise," said the Badger, "never to touch a motorcar again?"

"Certainly not!" replied Toad. "On the contrary, I promise that the very first motorcar I see, poop-poop! off I go in it!"

"Told you so, didn't I?" said the Rat to the Mole.

"Very well, then," said the Badger. "Since you won't yield to persuasion, we'll try what force can do. You've often asked us three to come and stay with you, Toad. Well, now we're going to."

"It's for your own good, Toady, you know," said the Rat.

"We'll take great care of everything for you till you're well, Toad," said the Mole; "and we'll see your money isn't wasted, as it has been."

"No more of these regrettable incidents with the police, Toad," said the Rat, as they thrust him into his bedroom and turned the key on him.

They went down the stairs, Toad shouting abuse at them through the keyhole.

"It's going to be a tedious business," said the Badger to Mole and Rat. "I've never seen Toad so determined. However, we will see it out. He must never be left an instant unguarded. We shall have to take it in turns to be with him till the poison has worked itself out of his system."

One fine morning the Rat, whose turn it was to go on duty, went upstairs to relieve Badger. "Toad's still in bed," Badger told the Rat. "Now, you look out. When Toad's quiet and obedient, then he's at his most cunning. There's sure to be something up." Then the Badger and Mole left for a long ramble round the wood and down tunnels.

"How are you today, old chap?" the Rat asked, as he approached Toad's bedside.

In a feeble voice, Toad replied, "Thank you so much, dear Ratty. I know you're tired of bothering about me. I mustn't ask you to do anything further."

"But I tell you," said the Rat, "I'd take any trouble on earth for you, if only you'd be a sensible animal."

"Then I would beg you—for the last time, probably— to step round to the village as quickly as possible— even now it may be too late—and fetch the doctor."

"Why, what do you want a doctor for?" asked the Rat, coming closer.

"I fear, dear friend," said Toad, with a sad smile, "that a doctor can do little in a case like this. Still, one must grasp at the slightest straw. And, by the way, I hate to give you additional trouble, but I happen to remember that while you're fetching the doctor you will pass the lawyer's door—would you mind at the same time asking him to step up?"

"A lawyer! O, he must be really bad!" the frightened Rat said to himself as he hurried from the room, not forgetting, however, to lock the door carefully behind him before he ran off to the village.

The Toad, who had hopped lightly out of bed as soon as he heard the key turned in the lock, watched Rat from the window till he disappeared down the driveway. Then, laughing, he dressed as quickly as

possible in the best suit he could find, filled his pockets with cash, and next, tying a rope to the divider in the window, he scrambled out, slid lightly to the ground, and, taking the opposite direction to the Rat, marched off, whistling a merry tune.

It was a gloomy lunch for Rat when the Badger and the Mole returned, and he had to face them with his story about how Toad had so easily tricked him.

"He's got clear away for the time," said Badger, "that's certain. And the worst of it is, he'll be so conceited with what he'll think is his cleverness that he may commit any folly. One comfort is, we're free now, and needn't waste any more of our precious time being guards. But we'd better continue to sleep at Toad Hall for a while longer. Toad may be brought back at any moment—on a stretcher, or between two policemen."

So spoke the Badger, not knowing what the future held in store before Toad should sit at ease again in Toad Hall.

Meanwhile, Toad was walking along the high road, miles from home.

He strode along, his head in the air, till he reached a little town and went into an inn and ordered lunch and sat down to eat it in the coffee room.

He was about halfway through his meal when a familiar sound, approaching down the street, made him start trembling all over. The poop-poop! drew nearer and nearer, the car could be heard to turn into the innyard and come to a stop. Soon the party entered the coffee room, hungry, talkative and happy. At last Toad could stand it no longer. He slipped out of the room quietly, paid his bill at the bar, and as soon as he got outside made his way to the innyard. "There cannot be any harm," he said to himself, "in my only just *looking* at it!"

Toad walked slowly round the car, inspecting it.

"I wonder," he said to himself, "if this sort of car *starts* easily?"

He found he had hold of the starting handle and was turning it. As the familiar sound broke forth, the old passion seized on Toad. As if in a dream he found himself seated in the driver's seat; as if in a dream, he swung the car round the yard and out through the archway; and, as if in a dream, all sense of right and wrong, all fear of consequences, seemed suspended. He increased his pace, and as the car devoured the street and leapt forth on the road through open country, he only felt that he was Toad once more. Toad at his best and highest, Toad the Terror. The miles were eaten up under him as he sped he knew not where, reckless of what might come to him.

Seemingly the next thing Toad knew, though it was hours later, he was in court before a judge.

"Let me see," said the judge. "He has been found guilty, first, of stealing a valuable motorcar; secondly, of driving to the public danger; and, thirdly, of rudeness and unruliness to the police. Mr. Clerk, will you tell us, please, what is the very stiffest penalty we can impose for each of these offenses?"

"If added up correctly," said the clerk, "nineteen years. But you had better make it a round twenty years and be on the safe side."

"An excellent suggestion!" said the judge.

The Toad was loaded with chains and dragged from the courthouse. He was taken to the grimmest dungeon in the strongest castle in all of Merry England.

7
Toad's Adventures

TOAD FLUNG himself on the floor and shed bitter tears. "This is the end of everything," he said. "At least it is the end of the career of Toad, which is the same thing; the popular and handsome Toad, the rich and hospitable Toad, the Toad so free and careless and elegant! How can I hope to be ever set free again after I have been imprisoned so justly for stealing so handsome a motorcar. Stupid animal that I was, now I must waste away in this dungeon, till people who were proud to say they knew me, have forgotten the very name of Toad! O wise old Badger! O clever, intelligent Rat and sensible Mole! O unhappy Toad!" He passed his days and nights for several weeks like this, refusing meals, though the grim, old jailer pointed out that many comforts could be sent in—at a price—from outside.

Now the jailer had a daughter, a pleasant, good-hearted girl. She was particularly fond of animals. This kind-hearted girl, pitying the misery of Toad, said to her father one day, "Father! I can't bear to see that poor beast so unhappy, and getting so thin! You let me have the managing of him."

Her father replied that she could do what she liked with him. He was tired of Toad. So that day she knocked at the door of Toad's cell.

"Now, cheer up, Toad," she said, "and sit up and dry your eyes and be a sensible animal. And do try and eat a bit of dinner. See, I've brought you some of mine, hot from the oven!"

It was cabbage and potatoes, and its fragrance filled the little cell. When Toad wailed and kicked with his legs and refused to be comforted, the wise girl went away with it for a while. But the smell of the hot cabbage remained behind, and Toad, between his sobs, began to think new thoughts: of deeds still to be done; of broad meadows; of the sound of dishes set down on the table at Toad Hall. And lastly, he thought of his own great cleverness and know-how, and all that he was capable of if he only gave his great mind to it; and the cure was almost complete.

When the girl returned hours later, she carried a tray, with a cup of fragrant tea on it; and a plate piled up with very hot buttered toast, cut thick, very brown on both sides, with the butter running through the holes in it in great golden drops, like honey from the honeycomb. The smell of that buttered toast simply talked to Toad; talked of warm kitchens, of breakfasts on bright, frosty mornings, of cozy parlor firesides on winter evenings. Toad sat up once more, dried his eyes, sipped his tea and munched his toast, and soon began talking freely about himself, and the house he lived in, and how important he was, and what a lot his friends thought of him.

"Tell me about Toad Hall," said she. "It sounds beautiful. But first wait till I fetch you some more tea and toast."

She hurried away and soon returned with a fresh trayful; and Toad, his spirits quite restored to their usual level, told her about the boathouse, and the fishpond, and the old walled kitchen garden; and about the pigsties, and the stables, and the pigeon house, and the henhouse; and about the dairy; and about the banqueting hall, and the fun they had there when the other animals were gathered round the table and Toad was at his best, singing songs, telling stories. Then she wanted to know about his animal friends, and was very interested in all he had to tell her about them and how they lived, and what they did to pass their time. When she said goodnight, Toad was very much the same self-satisfied animal that he had been of old. He sang a little song or two, curled himself up in the straw, and had an excellent night's rest and the pleasantest of dreams.

They had many interesting talks together, after that,

as the dreary days went on; and the jailer's daughter grew very sorry for Toad, and thought it a great shame that a poor little animal should be locked up in prison for what seemed to her a very trivial offence.

One morning the girl was very thoughtful, and did not seem to Toad to be paying proper attention to his witty sayings and sparkling comments.

"Toad," she said, "just listen, please. I have an aunt who is a washerwoman."

"There, there," said Toad, "never mind; think no more about it. *I* have several aunts who *ought* to be washerwomen."

"Do be quiet a minute, Toad," said the girl. "You talk too much, that's your chief fault, and I'm trying to think, and you hurt my head. As I said, I have an aunt who is a washerwoman; she does the washing for all the prisoners in this castle. Now, this is what occurs to me: you're very rich, and she's very poor. A little money wouldn't make any difference to you, and it would mean a lot to her. Now, I think if she were properly approached, you could come to some arrangement by which she would let you have her dress and bonnet, and you could escape from the castle as the official washerwoman. You're very alike in many respects—particularly about the figure."

"We're *not*," said the Toad. "I have a very elegant figure—for what I am."

"So has my aunt," said the girl, "for what *she* is. But have it your own way. You horrid, proud, ungrateful animal, when I'm sorry for you and trying to help you!"

"Yes, yes, that's all right; thank you very much indeed," said the Toad. "But look here! You wouldn't have Mr. Toad, of Toad Hall, going about the country disguised as a washerwoman!"

"Then you can stay here as a Toad," replied the girl. "I suppose you want to go off in a fancy carriage!"

Honest Toad was always ready to admit himself in the wrong. "You are a good, kind, clever girl," he said, "and I am indeed a proud and stupid toad. Introduce me to your aunt, if you will be so kind, and I have no doubt that the excellent lady and I will be able to arrange terms."

The next evening the girl brought her aunt into Toad's cell. In return for his cash, Toad received a cotton print gown, an apron, a shawl and a black bonnet.

When the girl dressed Toad, she giggled, "You're

the very image of her. Now, goodbye, Toad, and good
luck."

Toad set forth on what seemed to be a most
harebrained and hazardous journey. But he was soon
happily surprised to find how easy everything was
made for him. The washerwoman's squat figure in its
familiar cotton print seemed a passport for every
barred door and gateway.

It seemed hours before he crossed the last court-
yard, but at last he heard the gate in the great outer
door click behind him, felt the fresh air of the outer
world, and knew that he was free!

Dizzy with the success of his daring escape, he
walked quickly towards the lights of the town. He
made his way to the train station and found that a
train, bound more or less in the direction of his
home, was due to start in half an hour. "More luck!"
said Toad, and went off to the booking office to buy
his ticket. But here he found not only no money, but
no pocket to hold it! To his horror he remembered
that he had left his coat behind him in his cell, and
with it his money, keys, watch, matches, pencil
case—all that makes life worth living.

He made one desperate effort to carry the thing off,
and said, "Look here! I find I've left my purse behind.
Just give me that ticket, will you, and I'll send the
money on tomorrow. I'm well known in these parts."

The clerk laughed. "Here, stand away from the
window, please, madam," he said. "You're blocking
the other passengers."

Baffled and full of despair, he wandered down the platform where the train was standing, and tears trickled down each side of his nose. Very soon his escape would be discovered, the hunt would be up, he would be caught, loaded with chains, dragged back again to prison, and bread and water and straw; and O, what sarcastic remarks the girl would make! What was to be done? As he pondered he found himself opposite the engine and its driver, a burly man with an oilcan.

"Hullo, mother!" said the engine driver. "What's the trouble? You don't look particularly cheerful."

"O, sir!" said Toad, crying again. "I am a poor unhappy washerwoman, and I've lost all my money, and can't pay for a ticket, and I *must* get home tonight somehow, and whatever I am to do I don't know. O dear, O dear!"

"That's a bad business, indeed," said the engine driver. "Lost your money—and can't get home—and got some kids, too, waiting for you, I dare say?"

"Any number of them," sobbed Toad. "And they'll be hungry—and playing with matches—and upsetting lamps, the little innocents!—and quarreling, and going on generally. O dear, O dear!"

"Well, I'll tell you what I'll do," said the good engine driver. "You're a washerwoman. And I'm an engine driver, and there's no denying it's terribly dirty work. If you'll wash a few shirts for me when you get home, and send 'em along, I'll give you a ride on my engine."

Toad eagerly scrambled up into the cab of the engine. Of course Toad had never washed a shirt in his life, and couldn't if he tried, but he thought: "When I get safely home to Toad Hall, and have money again, and pockets to put it in, I will send the engine driver enough to pay for a lot of washing, and that will be the same thing, or better."

The train moved out of the station. As the speed increased, and the Toad could see on either side of him fields, and trees, and hedges, and cows, and horses, all flying past him, and as he thought how every minute was bringing him nearer to Toad Hall, he began to skip up and down and shout and sing, to the great astonishment of the driver.

They had covered many and many a mile, when Toad noticed that the driver was leaning over the side of the engine and listening hard. "It's very strange," said the driver. "We're the last train running in this direction tonight, yet I could be sworn that I heard another following us!"

The moon was shining brightly, and the driver soon took another look. "It seems as if we were being pursued! They are gaining on us fast! And the engine is crowded with policemen and jailers and detectives, all waving, all shouting the same thing—'Stop, stop, stop!'"

The Toad fell on his knees among the coals and, raising his clasped paws in prayer, cried, "Save me, dear kind Mr. Engine Driver, and I will confess everything! I am not the simple washerwoman I seem to be! I have no children waiting for me! I am a Toad— the well-known and popular Mr. Toad; I have just escaped, by my great daring and cleverness, from a loathsome dungeon into which my enemies had flung me; and if those fellows recapture me, it will be chains once more for poor, unhappy, innocent Toad!"

The engine driver looked down upon him and said, "Now tell me the truth; what were you put in prison for?"

"It was nothing very much," said poor Toad. "I only borrowed a motorcar while the owners were at lunch. I didn't mean to steal it, really; but people take such hard views of thoughtless and high-spirited actions."

The engine driver said, "I fear that you have been

indeed a wicked toad, but you are so much in distress, that I will not desert you. So cheer up, Toad! I'll do my best, and we may beat them yet!"

They piled on more coals, but still their pursuers slowly gained. The engine driver sighed, and said, "I'm afraid it's no good, Toad. You see, they have a better engine. There's just one thing left for us to do. A short way ahead of us is a long tunnel, and on the other side of that the line passes through a thick wood. When we are through the tunnel, I will shut off steam and put on brakes as hard as I can, and then you must jump and hide in the wood, before they get through the tunnel and see you. Then I will go full speed ahead again, and they can chase me if they like. Now mind and be ready to jump when I tell you!"

The train shot into the tunnel, and the engine rushed and roared and rattled, till at last they shot out at the other end into fresh air and saw the wood lying dark upon either side of the line. The driver put on brakes, and as the train slowed down to almost a walking pace, Toad heard the driver call out, "Now, jump!"

Toad jumped, rolled down a short embankment, picked himself up, scrambled into the wood and hid.

When the pursuing train had passed, the Toad had a hearty laugh. But he soon stopped laughing when he came to consider that it was now very late and dark and cold, and he was in an unknown wood, and still far from home.

At last, cold, hungry and tired out, he found the shelter of a hollow tree, where with branches and dead leaves he made himself as comfortable a bed as he could, and slept soundly till morning.

8

The Further Adventures of Toad

TOAD WOKE up early that next morning after his escape—early because of the coldness of his toes, which made him dream that he was at home in bed on a cold winter's night, and his blankets and sheets had got up, grumbling that they couldn't stand the cold any longer, and had run downstairs to the kitchen fire to warm themselves; and he had followed, on bare feet, along miles and miles of icy stone-paved floors, arguing with them and asking them to be reasonable.

Sitting up, he rubbed his eyes first and his complaining toes next, wondered for a moment where he was, then remembered everything—that he was free!

He shook himself and brushed the dry leaves off his head with his fingers. Still dressed as a washer-woman, he then marched forth into the morning sun and reached the road. A canal ran alongside the road for a time, and Toad followed along the towpath a horse that was towing behind it a canal boat.

The only person on the barge was a big stout woman wearing a sunbonnet.

"A nice morning, ma'am," she remarked to Toad.

"I dare say it is, ma'am!" responded Toad politely,

as he walked along the towpath. "I dare say it is a nice morning to them that's not in sore trouble, like what I am. I've left my laundering business to look after itself while I go to my married daughter; and I've lost all my money, and lost my way."

"Where might your married daughter be living, ma'am?" asked the barge woman.

"She lives near to the river, ma'am," replied Toad. "Close to a fine house called Toad Hall."

"Toad Hall? Why, I'm going that way myself," said the barge woman. "You come along in the barge with me, and I'll give you a lift."

Toad thanked her and stepped aboard.

"So you're in the washing business, ma'am?" said the barge woman.

"Finest business in the whole country," said Toad. "All the rich folks come to me. You see, I understand my work thoroughly. Everything's done under my own eye!"

"And are you very fond of washing?"

"I love it," said Toad. "Never so happy as when I've got both arms in a washtub. But, then, it comes so easy to me! A real pleasure, I assure you, ma'am!"

"What a bit of luck, meeting you!" said the barge woman. "There's a heap of things of mine that you'll find in a corner of the cabin. If you'll just take one or two of the most necessary sort and put them through the washtub as we go along, why, it'll be a pleasure to you, and a real help to me."

"If it comes to that," Toad thought, "I suppose any fool can *wash!*"

A long half-hour passed, and every minute of it saw Toad getting crosser and crosser. Nothing that he could do to the clothes seemed to please them or do them good.

A burst of laughter made him straighten his sore back and look round. The barge woman was laughing till the tears ran down her cheeks.

"I've been watching you all the time," she gasped. "What a washerwoman you are!"

Toad lost his temper. "You common, low, *fat* barge woman!" he shouted. "Washerwoman indeed! I would have you to know that I am a Toad, a very well-known, respected Toad!"

The woman moved closer to him and peered under his bonnet. "Why, so you are!" she cried. "A horrid, nasty, crawly Toad! And in my nice clean barge, too! Now that is a thing I will *not* have."

She caught Toad by a foreleg, then the world turned suddenly upside down to him, and Toad found himself flying through the air. The water, which he reached with a loud splash, was cold enough. He rose to the surface spluttering, and the first thing he saw was the fat barge woman looking back at him over the back of the boat and laughing.

When he got to shore, he ran after the barge along the towpath as fast as his legs and the wet heavy clothes would allow him.

The barge woman was still laughing when he drew up level with her.

He saw what he wanted as revenge ahead of him. He overtook the horse, unfastened the towrope and

cast off, jumped on the horse's back, and urged it to a gallop.

The horse soon slowed to a walk, but Toad was happy, knowing that he was moving and the barge was not. He left the canal miles behind him.

The horse came to a stop to nibble some grass. Near them was a Gypsy caravan, and beside it was a man sitting on an upside-down bucket and smoking and staring into the wide world. A fire of sticks was burning near by, and over the fire hung an iron pot, and out of that pot came forth bubblings and gurglings—and warm, rich and varied smells.

Toad sat on the horse and sniffed and sniffed, and looked at the Gypsy; and the Gypsy sat and smoked and looked at him.

Soon the Gypsy took his pipe out of his mouth and said, "Want to sell that there horse of yours?"

It had not occurred to Toad to turn the horse into cash, but this suggestion seemed to smooth the way towards the two things Toad wanted so badly—money and a solid breakfast.

"What?" said Toad, "me sell this beautiful young horse of mine? O, no; it's out of the question. Who's going to take the washing home to my customers every week? No, it's not to be thought of for a moment. All the same, how much might you be disposed to offer me for this beautiful young horse of mine?"

The Gypsy looked the horse over, and then he looked Toad over, and looked at the horse again.

"A shilling a leg," he said.

"A shilling a leg?" cried Toad. "If you please, I must take a little time to work that out, and see just what it comes to."

He climbed down off his horse, and did sums on his fingers and at last said, "A shilling a leg? Why, that comes to exactly four shillings, and no more. O, no; I could not think of accepting four shillings for this beautiful young horse of mine."

"Well," said the Gypsy, "I'll tell you what I will do. I'll make it five shillings. And that's my last word."

Then Toad sat and thought. At last he said, "This is my last word. You shall hand me over six shillings and sixpence; and further, you shall give me as much breakfast as I can possibly eat out of that iron pot of yours. In return, I will make over to you my young horse. If that's not good enough for you, say so, and

I'll be getting on. I know a man near here who's wanted this horse of mine for years."

The Gypsy grumbled but finally paid Toad. Then he brought out a large plate and a knife, fork and spoon for him. It was, indeed, the most beautiful stew in the world. Toad took the plate on his lap and stuffed and stuffed and stuffed. He thought he had never eaten so good a breakfast in all his life.

The Gypsy gave Toad good directions towards the riverside, and Toad tramped along happily. "Ho, ho!" he said to himself as he marched along with his chin in the air. "What a clever Toad I am! There is surely no animal equal to me in the whole world! My enemies shut me up in prison; I walk out through all the guards. They chase me; I vanish. I am thrown into a canal by a woman. What of it? I swim ashore, steal her horse, and ride off in triumph, and I sell the horse for a whole pocketful of money. Ho, ho! I am The Toad, the handsome, the popular, the successful Toad!" He made up a song as he walked in praise of himself, and sang it at the top of his voice, though there was no one to hear it but him. It was perhaps the most conceited song that any animal ever composed:

> The world has had great heroes,
> As history books have showed;
> But never a name to go down to fame
> Compared with that of Toad!
>
> The Queen and her Ladies-in-waiting
> Sat at the window and sewed.

She cried, "Look! who's that *handsome* man?"
They answered, "Mr. Toad."

There was a great deal more of the same sort, but too dreadfully conceited to be written down. These are some of the milder verses.

He sang as he walked, and he walked as he sang, and got more inflated every minute. But his pride was shortly to have a great fall.

After miles of country lanes he reached the high road, and as he got onto it, he glanced along its length, and saw approaching him something very familiar.

"This is once more the great world from which I have been missed so long!" he said. He stepped out into the road to hail the motorcar. But suddenly he felt sick inside. The approaching car was the very one he had stolen on that day when all his troubles began! And the people in it were the same!

He sank down in a heap on the road, murmuring to himself, "It's all over now! Chains and policemen again! Prison again! O, what a fool I have been!"

The terrible car drew near and stopped. Two gentlemen got out and walked round Toad. "O dear! This is very sad! Here is a poor old thing—a washer-woman—who has fainted in the road! Let us lift her into the car and take her to the nearest village."

They lifted Toad and put him in their car and went on their way.

Toad opened his eyes.

"Look!" said one of the gentlemen. "The fresh air is doing her good. How do you feel now, ma'am?"

"I'm feeling a great deal better!" Toad sat up, looked about him, and tried to beat down the old cravings that rose up and took hold of him.

"Please, sir," he said to the gentleman driving, "I wish you would let me try and drive the car a little."

The driver laughed, and the other gentleman said, "Bravo, ma'am! I like your spirit. Let her have a try," he said to the driver. "She won't do any harm."

Toad listened to the instructions given him, and set the car in motion, very slowly at first.

The gentlemen, now sitting behind him, clapped their hands, and Toad heard them saying, "How well she does it!"

Toad went a little faster; then faster still, and faster.

He heard the gentlemen call out, "Be careful, washerwoman!"

The driver tried to interfere, but Toad went on full speed. The rush of the air in his face, the hum of the engines and the jump of the car made his weak brain dizzy. "Washerwoman, indeed!" he shouted. "Ho! ho! I am the Toad, the car snatcher, the prison breaker, the Toad who always escapes!"

The gentlemen grabbed him, but with a half-turn of the wheel the Toad sent the car crashing through the low hedge along the roadside. There was one mighty bound, and then the wheels of the car were churning up the mud of a horse pond.

Toad found himself flying through the air like a bird before he landed with a thump in the soft grass of a meadow. Sitting up, he could see the car in the pond, nearly under water; the gentlemen were in the water.

Toad picked himself up and set off running till he was out of breath and had to settle down into a walk. When he had recovered his breath, he began to giggle. Then he burst into song again—

The motorcar went Poop-poop-poop,
    As it raced along the road.
Who was it steered it into a pond?
    Ingenious Mr. Toad!

"O, how clever I am! How—"

A noise at a distance made him turn his head and look. O horror! About two fields off, he could see two policemen and the gentlemen running towards him!

Poor Toad sprang to his feet and ran away again. "O, my!" he gasped, "what a fool I am! Shouting and singing again! O, my!"

On he ran desperately, but they still gained on him. He did his best, but he was a fat animal, and his legs were short. Not even looking where he was going, the earth failed under his feet, he grasped at the air and, splash! he found himself head over ears in deep water, rapid water, water that bore him along. He had run straight into the river!

The stream was so strong that he couldn't hold on to the reeds by the water's edge. "O my!" gasped poor Toad. "If ever I steal a car again! If ever I sing another conceited song!" Soon he saw that he was nearing a big dark hole in the bank. He reached up with a paw and caught hold of the edge and held on. Then slowly he drew himself up out of the water. As he puffed and panted and stared before him into the dark hole, some bright small thing twinkled inside and moved towards him. As it came, a face grew up around the twinkling, and it was a familiar face!

Brown and small, with whiskers. Round, with neat ears and silky hair.

It was the Water Rat!

9

Toad Hall Recaptured

TOAD WAS happy now that he had found himself once more in the house of a friend. "O, Ratty!" he cried. "I've been through such times since I saw you last! Such sufferings! Then such escapes! Been in prison—got out of it, of course. Been thrown into a canal—swam ashore! Stole a horse—sold him for a large sum of money! Tricked everybody! Oh, I am a smart Toad—"

"Toad," said the Water Rat, "you go off upstairs and take off that dress that looks as if it belonged to some washerwoman, and clean yourself, and put on some of my clothes, and try and come down looking like a gentleman."

Toad did so, and when he came down lunch was on the table. While they ate Toad told the Rat all his adventures. When at last Toad had talked himself silent, the Rat said, "Now, Toady, don't you see what an awful fool you've been making of yourself? And all because you had to go and steal a car. Why choose to be a convict? When are you going to be sensible, and think of your friends? Do you suppose it's any pleasure to me to hear animals saying that I'm the chap that keeps company with jailbirds?"

While the Rat was talking so seriously, Toad kept saying to himself, "But it was fun, though! Awful fun!" Yet when the Rat had quite finished, he said, very nicely, "Quite right, Ratty! Yes, I've been a conceited old fool, I can see that. But now I'm going to be a good Toad, and not do it anymore. Now, let's stroll down to Toad Hall, so I may get into clothes of my own, and set things going again on the old lines."

"Stroll down to Toad Hall?" cried the Rat. "Do you mean to say you haven't *heard* about the Stoats and Weasels?"

"What, the Wild Wooders?" cried Toad.

"They've taken Toad Hall!" said the Rat.

A large tear welled up in each of Toad's eyes. "Go on," said Toad, "tell me all."

"When you—got—into that—car trouble of yours," said the Rat slowly, "well, it was a good deal talked about down here, not only along the riverside, but even in the Wild Wood. The River-bankers stuck up for you, but the Wild Wood animals said hard things, that it served you right, and it was time this sort of thing was stopped. They went about saying you were done for this time, that you would never come back again, never, never! Mole and Badger moved their things to Toad Hall to have it all ready for you when you returned. They didn't guess what was going to happen. One dark night, a band of weasels, armed to the teeth, crept up to the front entrance. At the same time ferrets advanced through the garden, while stoats came in through the windows. The Mole and Badger made the best fight they could, but what could two animals do against hundreds? And the Wild Wooders have been living in Toad Hall ever since!"

"O, have they!" said Toad.

The Badger and the Mole, who had been checking up on the Wild Wooders' activities in Toad Hall every day since being thrown out, soon returned to Rat's hole and greeted Toad. Toad was eager to tell them about his adventures, but Badger preferred to present his plan for retaking Toad Hall.

"There's going to be a big banquet tomorrow night," said Badger. "It's the Chief Weasel's birthday, and all the weasels will be gathered together in the dining hall, eating and drinking and laughing and carrying on, suspecting nothing. No guns, no swords, no sticks. That very useful tunnel from my den into Toad Hall leads right up under the butler's pantry, next to the dining hall."

"We shall creep out into the butler's pantry—" cried the Mole.

"—and rush in upon them," said the Badger.

"—and whack 'em, and whack 'em, and whack 'em!" cried the Toad.

"Very well, then," said the Badger. "Our plan is settled."

The next night, when it began to grow dark, the Badger led the Mole, the Rat and Toad along the river for a little way, and then into a hole in the river bank. They were in the secret passage, and the expedition had really begun!

It was cold, and dark, and damp, and low, and narrow, and poor Toad began to shiver. Finally, Badger said, "We ought by now to be pretty nearly under the Hall."

They heard, over their heads, a confused murmur of sound, as if people were shouting and cheering and stamping on the floor and hammering on tables. The Badger remarked, "They are going at it, those Weasels!"

The passage now began to slope upwards; and then the noise broke out again. "Ooo-ray-oo-ray-oo-ray-oo-ray!" they heard.

"Come on!" said the Badger to his friends. Such a noise was going on in the banqueting hall that there was little danger of their being overheard as they popped up through the trapdoor into the pantry.

They could now clearly hear the weasels' voices.

"Get ready, all of you!" said Badger. "The hour is come! Follow me!"

He flung the door into the dining hall wide open My!

What a squealing and a squeaking and a screeching filled the air!

The terrified weasels dove under the tables in panic when the four heroes strode into the room! They were but four in all, but to the panic-stricken weasels the hall seemed full of monstrous animals, gray, black, brown and yellow, with enormous sticks; and the weasels fled with squeals of terror and dismay, this way and that, through the windows, up the chimney, anywhere to get out of reach of those terrible sticks. In five minutes the room was cleared.

After all the unwelcome guests had escaped across the lawn, the Badger said, "I want some grub, I do. Stir yourself, Toad. We've got your house back for you, and you don't offer us so much as a sandwich."

Toad and the others found plenty of food for a feast. So they had their supper in great joy and contentment, and then went off to sleep, safe in Toad's family home, won back by bravery, planning and sticks.

In the morning the Badger reminded his host that Toad had to host a banquet that night to celebrate the recapture of Toad Hall.

Toad thought the banquet would give him the chance to brag about his adventures to all his riverbank friends, but Rat understood what was going

through Toad's head, and told him, "We want you to understand clearly, once and for all, that there are going to be no speeches and no songs. We're not arguing with you; we're just telling you."

"Mayn't I sing them just one *little* song?" he pleaded.

"No, not *one* little song," replied the Rat. "It's no good, Toady; you know that your songs are all conceit and boasting and vanity; and your speeches are self-praise. You know you must turn over a new leaf sooner or later, and now seems a splendid time to begin."

"You have conquered me, my friends," Toad said. "You are right. From now on I will be a very different Toad. But, O dear, O dear, this is a hard world!"

Pressing his handkerchief to his face, he left the room.

"Badger," said the Rat, "*I* feel like a brute."

"O, I know, I know," said the Badger. "But the thing had to be done."

That night, near the time for the banquet, Toad locked himself in his room, and sang a song to himself:

> The Toad—came—home!
> There was panic in the parlor and howling in
>   the hall,
> There was crying in the cowshed and shriek-
>   ing in the stall,
> When the Toad—came—home!

When the Toad—came—home!
There was smashing in of window and
    crashing in of door,
There was chasing after weasels that fainted
    on the floor,
When the Toad—came—home!

Bang! go the drums!
The trumpeters are tooting and the soldiers
    are saluting,
And the cannon they are shooting and the
    motorcars are hooting,
As the—Hero—comes!

Shout—Hooray!
And let each one of the crowd try and shout
    it very loud,
In honor of an animal of whom you're justly
    proud,
For it's Toad's—great—day!

He sang this very loud, and when he had done, he sang it all over again. Then he heaved a deep sigh. Then he unlocked the door and went down the stairs to greet his guests.

All the animals cheered when he entered, and crowded round to congratulate him and say nice things about his courage, and his cleverness, and his fighting qualities, but Toad only smiled, and murmured, "Not at all!" Or, sometimes, for a change, "On the contrary!"

The animals were puzzled by this unexpected attitude of his.

The Badger had ordered everything of the best, and the banquet was a great success. When the younger animals encouraged Toad to make a speech or sing a song, Toad only shook his head and changed the subject. He was indeed a changed Toad!

After this night, the four animals continued to lead their lives, undisturbed by more fights or invasions. Toad, after talk with his friends, selected a gold chain and pearls, which he sent to the jailer's daughter with a letter; and the engine driver was thanked and paid back for all his pains and trouble. Even the barge woman was found and the value of her horse was returned to her.

Sometimes, in the course of long summer evenings, the friends would take a stroll together in the Wild

Wood, now tamed so far as they were concerned; and it was pleasing to see how respectfully they were greeted by the animals living there, and how the mother weasels would bring their young ones to the mouths of their holes, and say, pointing, "Look, baby! There goes the great Mr. Toad! And that's the gallant Water Rat, a terrible fighter! And here comes the famous Mr. Mole!" When their weasel children were naughty and out of control, the mothers would quiet them by telling how, if they didn't hush up, the terrible gray Badger would get them. This was a mean and unfair thing to say of Badger, who, though he cared little about the world, was rather fond of children; but it never failed to have its full effect.

THE END.